TWO SPECKLED EGGS

Jennifer K. Mann

WALKER BOOKS
AND SUBSIDIARIES
LONDON · BOSTON · SYDNEY · AUCKLAND

GINGER'S BIRTHDAY PARTY was in two weeks
and she wanted to invite all the girls in her class ...

except Lyla Browning.

Lyla Browning was weird: she smelled like old leaves, she didn't talk much, and she even brought a tarantula in a pickle jar for Show-and-Tell.

But Ginger's mum said she had to invite all the girls
in her class – or none of them.

Since "none of them" wouldn't be a very fun birthday party,
Ginger invited all of them – even Lyla Browning.

When the doorbell rang on the day of the party, Ginger ran to answer it.

It was Lyla Browning. She was very early.

Eventually, the doorbell rang again – and then again and again and again.

The girls piled their presents on the table,
then ran off to play the party games.

But Ava changed all the rules
to Blind Man's Bluff.

And Caroline dropped the egg
for the egg-and-spoon race before
it even started.

Then Maya and Julia stuck all the tails for Pin the Tail
on the Donkey on each other.

"You're spoiling all the games!" yelled Ginger.
But the girls had already started the three-legged race.

Finally it was time for silver-and-gold cake, Ginger's favourite. But Maggie didn't like coconut and Sara wouldn't eat the pineapple part. The rest of the girls just picked at the frosting and didn't touch the cake.

Except Lyla Browning.

Maybe "none of them" would have been a better party after all, Ginger thought as the girls ran off, giggling. She scrunched up her eyes, but the tears fell out anyway.

Just then something landed on Ginger's nose – a ladybird!
Ginger crossed her eyes to look at it.

Lyla Browning laughed. So did Ginger.

At last it was time for presents.
Ginger opened them one by one.

Lyla Browning's was the last present.

Ginger opened the flaps of the brown box and
pulled out what looked like a tiny bird's nest.

Lyla had made it herself, she said, out of paper, tinsel, ribbon and string. In the centre were two speckled eggs.

"They're chocolate – caramel cream!" Lyla whispered.

"Oh!" gasped Ginger. "I love caramel-cream eggs!"

"Me too," said Lyla.

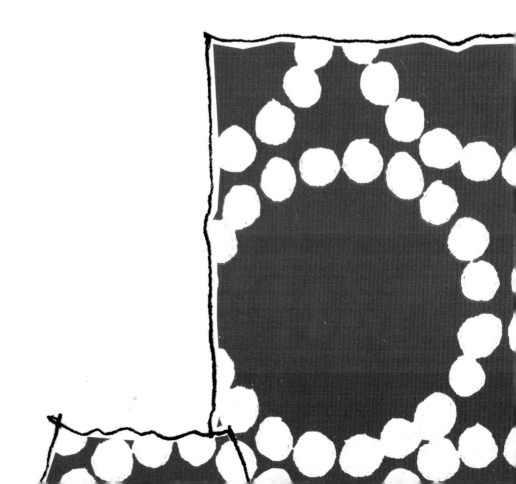

Later, when everyone else had gone, Ginger gave Lyla one of the eggs.

Then Ginger and Lyla pretended they were birds and pecked at the rest of the birthday cake until Lyla had to go home.

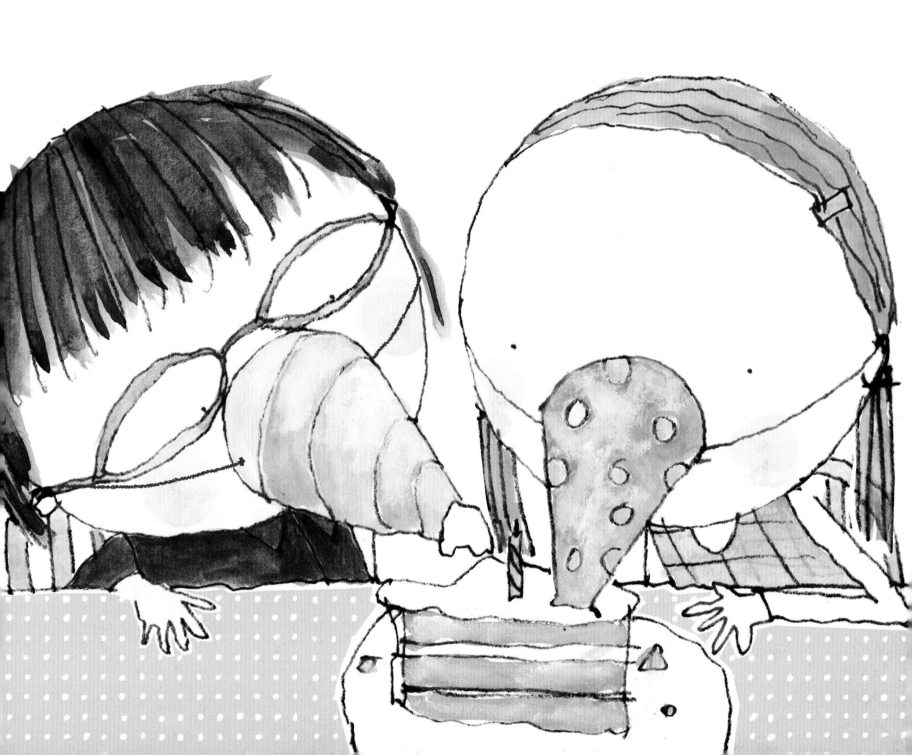

No one else carried a magnifying glass in her pocket
or made bird's nests for birthday presents.

And no one else knew that silver-and-gold cake and
two speckled eggs could make a birthday perfect.

Except Lyla Browning … and Ginger.

For S. D. G.,
cake-maker, memory-keeper, cheerleader, mom.
Wish you were here to see this.

First published 2014 by Walker Books Ltd
87 Vauxhall Walk, London SE11 5HJ

© 2014 Jennifer K. Mann

British Library Cataloguing in Publication Data:
a catalogue record for this book is available from the British Library

This book has been typeset in Caecilia

2 4 6 8 10 9 7 5 3 1

Printed in China

ISBN 978-1-4063-5153-8

www.walker.co.uk